Snow in Amman

An Anthology of Short Stories from Jordan

Translated and Edited by
Ibtihal Mahmood
Alexander Haddad

First published in 2015 by
FARAXA

Published by
FARAXA Publishing
38 Antonio Nani Street, Rabat RBT 3047, Malta; and
P. O. Box 37, East Longmeadow, MA 01020, USA.
http://faraxapublishing.com
info@faraxapublishing.com

ISBN 978-9995748-16-6

Printed in the United States of America.

To Donna

Acknowledgments

This anthology owes its existence to the assistance of many wonderful authors. I must express my heartfelt appreciation to the authors who granted me written permission to translate and publish selections from their works in this volume.

Locating the authors and collecting the stories for translation could not have been possible without the assistance of the author Samir Al-Sharif, who went out of his way to facilitate the communication between the other authors and myself. He let them know about my desire to translate an anthology of short stories from Jordan and sent me the works they wished to be included in this anthology.

CONTENTS

THE JORDANIAN SHORT STORY
Origins and Outcomes

Narration is natural. It has been hardwired into us for as long as *Homo sapiens* have been a species. Globally and regionally, we celebrate knights and maidens, adventurers, tricksters. The Arabian Nights are not just Scheherazade's nights; they are everyone's nights. Whole generations still hear the fables of Sayf ibn Dhi-Yazan echoing in their heads. Yet for all its rich, classical underpinnings, the modern short story in Arabic owes a great deal to its counterpart in the European tradition. It is an exchange from which both parties, no doubt, have benefited greatly.

Sources tracing the roots of the modern literary movement of Jordan tend to situate its origins in the works of Khalil Baidas and Mohammad Subhi Abu Ghanimeh, whose works appeared in the beginning of the 20th century. Their work was carried on from the 1930s by Mahmoud Seif ed-Din al-Irani, a formidable writer of short stories. His works were characterized by a once-upon-a-time resonance and a pronounced folklorishness. Indeed, this was the dominant style of Jordanian short fiction in the 1930s and '40s – a dominance that, in the opinion of this author, worked negatively upon the artistic value of those stories.

Both technically and objectively, one may consider the 1950s as the decade in which the modern Jordanian short story was born. This period witnessed a significant transformation in the intellectual and creative life of Jordan, spurred on by a wave of social upheaval and its concomitant explosion of political parties and attendant schools of thought. We may also look to the 1948 Arab-Israeli War and the resulting expulsion of Palestinians into

Jordan and other neighboring countries as a major factor shaping the consciousness of the modern Arab writer. This influx of heretofore peripheral groups into the heart of Jordanian society changed the way Jordanians conceived of space, culture and identity. It changed the parameters of both socioeconomic development and Jordan itself, turning its refugee-infused culture into a ferment of moral suffering and intellectual rigor.

It was the 1950s that laid the groundwork for the immense variety of aesthetic experimentation that took place in the following decade. If one accepts the claim that the '50s saw the birth of the modern Jordanian short story, we can rightly say that the 1960s constituted the decade of its rather tumultuous adolescence.

In Jordan as elsewhere, the 1960s saw the widespread dismantling and reconstruction of the short story as a distinct art form. This was a generation emblematized by pioneering writers like Mahmoud Shukair and Jamal Abu Hamdan, who took novel approaches to storytelling through symbolism, allegory, abstraction and a deep concern for the underlying metaphysical dilemma (i.e., What is reality – really?) posed by modern narrative fiction.

Out of this frenzy of artistic invention and reinvention there was one publication, *The New Horizon*, which bears particular mention. From 1961 to 1965, this periodical – much more than a periodical – was a perpetually churning dynamo of Arabic fiction, poetry and criticism: at once the beating heart and the far-flung messenger of the nascent literary movement of Jordan. Under the direction of the poet and novelist Amin Shinnar, *The New Horizon* brought a new generation of talented writers into the public eye.

On to the 1970s where the Jordanian short story truly came of age. Even to the casual reader, the shifts in attitude and tenor are unmistakable: it was the sound of a country finding its voice. The writings were of a mature literary culture, forged in a smithy of innumerable sufferings. Frustration and sadness, alienation and betrayal, were the prevailing themes in the stories of this period: echoes of the defeat in the 1967 war with Israel, the end of the resistance and the host of internal upheavals sweeping the region. The short stories of the '70s were more measured in their experimental tendencies, more confined in scale, than those of the preceding decade. The writers of this period concerned themselves chiefly with the expression of the local and the personal (the hyper-local) and the myriad distinctions that characterized them.

Jordanian literature in the 1980s and '90s witnessed further developments along this trajectory, keeping pace with the host of sociopolitical issues confronting Jordan, Palestine and the greater Arab World. The writings of this period unflinchingly examined the consequences engendered by the seemingly endless procession of conflicts across the region: civil war in Lebanon, the ascendance of Zionism in Israel, the Palestinian Intifada, the Iran-Iraq War, the Gulf War. Many authors of this period were women. This marked a new narrative direction in Jordanian literature, a clear departure from what had been a heavily male-dominated literary culture. Although many of these women have since (regrettably) chosen to withdraw from the public sphere, their contribution to Jordanian letters was of inestimable value.

Jordanian authors, particularly those who write and publish short stories, tend to overwhelmingly favor non-traditional avenues of publication. This despite the presence of public and private institutions dedicated to increasing the availability of publication opportunities for writers living in Jordan, such as the Jordanian Ministry of Culture, the Jordanian Writers Association and the Greater Amman Municipality. These institutions, although well meaning, have clearly been unable to keep pace with the ambitions of Jordanian writers and the groundswell of Jordan's burgeoning literary community. In the absence of a national publishing house, many authors have fallen susceptible to the whims of unethical publishers. Equally distressing is the utter failure of literary criticism in Jordan to measure up to the recent explosion of published works. Nowhere is this absence more grievously felt than in the sphere of academic criticism – apart from a few selective cases which, somewhat ironically, have been preoccupied with the deterioration of meaningful criticism in Jordanian letters.

This anthology, *Snow in Amman*, represents yet another step in the continuing journey of the Jordanian short story. Its pages contain multitudes: authors young and old, emerging and established, male and female, each with their own perspectives and experiences. In this way, the book you are holding is a panoramic view of the literary scene in Jordan today. It is my hope that other, similar initiatives will follow.

Many thanks to Ibtihal Mahmood and Alexander Haddad for their efforts in translating these stories. May the literary voice of Jordan find continued expression in English, no matter how far-flung its messengers.

Samir al-Sharif
Amman, Jordan

Why Jordanian Literature?

Because this translator is from Jordan. I spent 17 years of my life in Amman. Certainly, this is the most obvious answer, but also the most romanticized. I have many more reasons for undertaking this translation of 11 short stories by contemporary Jordanian authors. Some are less apparent, but all are important.

Jordan is a country with a rich history dating back to the Paleolithic. Some of the earliest written language was pioneered in the ancient civilizations of Jordan. I found it quite alarming to see a paucity of contemporary Jordanian literature available for the English-speaking public. Perhaps this has something to do with the general underrepresentation of Jordanian literature on the world stage: in a list of 105 best, Arabic-language novels of the 20th century selected by the Arab Writers Union, Jordan only appeared three times. By contrast, Egypt took the lion's share with 29 titles. To be fair, Egypt is a much larger country with a comparatively dense, urban population. But the literary tradition of Jordan is no less rich than that of Egypt. This begs the question: why not Jordanian literature?

As I understood the extent to which Jordan is underrepresented in the world of literature, especially literature in translation, I felt my inner philologist becoming restless. Translation, it is true, lies at the core of my academic training and focus. But at a more basic level, for myself the act of translating literature is one of the great joys in life. Literature in translation is one of the purest channels of intercultural communication, a thing of incredible importance in any age.

In choosing the pieces to include in this anthology, I made it a mission to seek out Jordanian works that avoided the Orientalizing influence that has become such a destructive cliché among works of Arabic fiction in translation. Enough has been said about tents and camels, virgins in veils, starry nights in the Sahara. Instead of focusing on the "otherness" of the Other, I was on the lookout for works that celebrated those aspects of being human which, despite the twin barriers of language and culture, remain ultimately universal. I am delighted to have gathered such a representative selection in *Snow in Amman*. These 11 stories capture, in a multitude of facets, the sort of universal perspectives I was hoping to find. It is a quality that complements, not overpowers, their distinctly Jordanian flavor.

As for the translation process, I made every effort to convey the intended meaning accurately and honestly, while maintaining the spirit and style of the original text, bearing in mind the formidable syntactic, semantic and stylistic differences between the source language, Arabic, and the target language, English. I think the resulting text reads as naturally as possible for an English-language reader.

Literary translation is a tough business: it is often referred to as a form of treason. There exists a fine line between breathing new life into a translated text and performing mere resuscitation. On the one hand, it is an honest rendering of the uniqueness of art. On the other hand, it is a blind and ultimately dishonest transportation of lexica from one language to another. It is my great hope that readers will find this work on the side of honesty.

Ibtihal Mahmood
Seattle, Washington

14

Snow in Amman

An Anthology of Short Stories from Jordan

TO MAKE A LIVING

Samir al-Sharif

When the car pulled over, he sprang off the pavement toward it, thrusting his head through a wide window to ask:

"Do you need a tile-setter? I'm a professional, a real craftsman, 20 years in the business. Name any building in the city – chances are that I've worked on it. And I won't," he said hurriedly, seeing the back seat fill with construction workers, "I won't take any pay until the job is finished."

The driver uttered something he could not understand. Then the wheels roared and the car sped away, stranding him in a cloud of his own stupefaction. He shuffled back to his patch of pavement and sat down to think.

You loiter at the holiday's threshold. In just a few hours' time, you'll stand before your host, facing his judgment. What preparations have you made? Do you think your family doesn't know how ill-equipped you are? You think, I'll keep a hold on myself. When the children come begging me for candy, I won't snarl at them. I'll be stern but fair. *Good – you try that. They'll keep begging anyway.*

The holidays arrive, always like a flock of arrows, striking old wounds and rending them anew. Not that you've had much of a chance to heal during the intervening year. Life gets in the way and besides, you know you can't afford to take time recuperating.

17

What of your meager wages have you squirrelled away, just so that you can put something into the hands of your sisters? What can you give them to appease the armies of children that hold them hostage? And what about your own children who regard the lamb in your neighbor's kitchen with heartbroken longing?

Perhaps God will have some mercy on you. Perhaps you'll go to your sisters' houses only to find that they've left. It would certainly save you a lot of trouble.

This year, you won't hesitate to buy your wife a new dress. She could use a new one: admit it. The old thing she's been wearing has turned into a field of snags and patchwork; a map of your own shelled-out marriage. Get her a new dress and it'll send her a signal, loud and clear, that your treachery – which you could never fully obfuscate – is at an end. You'll tell her (without having to tell her), Thank you for the graciousness you've shown.

But who knows? Even this plan could backfire. She might see dollar signs where there are none, asking you for a new pair of shoes – even though you bought her new ones just last year! You've seen it happen: once greed seeps into the heart, it's all over.

* * * * *

A commotion brought him back from himself. Other men were yelling: another car had come. He rapidly collected his tools, then hopped over to rest his foot on the rear of the car.

"Enough," the driver yelled.

He scoffed and spat, looking daggers at the foreman, then sauntered back to his parcel of pavement and squatted.

18

Pig-headed, he admonished himself. *You say you're trying to feed the hungry mouths around you, but look at what's come of your effort. Time turns its back on you.*

Look at your situation now. When you applied for that 'watchman' position, the foreman made it entirely clear that your only job there would be not to watch. *What kind of job is that, to let a few bags of cement walk from the yard each night? You did the right thing, passing up that offer.*

You need to prioritize. The holidays are around the corner again. Last year, your wife bristled because you didn't visit her mother at the cemetery. Inappropriate negligence, she told you, of the mother-in-law who propped you up through your poverty and who did so even when she had to hide it from her own husband.

Go to the cemetery. It'll silence your wife, at least on that particular subject. You should also see to repairing your father's grave: its crumbling face is barely legible these days.

You wonder if you're going crazy. But if everyone around him drinks daily from the river of madness, how does a man gauge his own sanity?

You wonder if you might be better off dead. But only dead fish go with the flow and the only way you know is to struggle against the current.

Talk about pain all you like, but it's not the same as feeling it.

He looked at his watch, reading the time with indifference. Its two hands hovered over the 10. Hunger struck him unbidden; the smell of a nearby *tabun*[1] ignited his imagination. He scanned the yard with cloudy eyes, flipped a coin and regarded it in his hand. A sigh sprouted from his chest. He surveyed his tools with a sense of enmity. He wanted to hurl them away from him, but the yard was full to bursting with men, their ceaseless chatter filling whatever empty spaces remained.

Suddenly, he felt someone pressing against him, pushing him toward a truck that had pulled into the yard. A voice said firmly:

"Get in."

He leaned against the rail, reading the desperation etched on the faces around him. Someone he could not see was muttering:

"It's because of all the foreign workers that we're reduced to this."

He stood up, staggering against the mass of people crowded into the truck bed, and found himself being supported by rough hands. He shouted:

"I'm NOT a foreign worker!"

The cry diffused into the air, supplanted by the roar of an engine. As the truck pulled out of the yard, he felt the eyes of all the men upon him. Their gaze formed a single question mark, wrapping and tightening about his neck like a noose.

---

[1] A clay oven, shaped like a truncated cone, with an opening at the bottom from which to stoke a fire.

THE CELLAR
[*Secrets of the Hourglass*, Chapter 1]
Elias Farkouh

The whole place was the very embodiment of disorder, but their presence did not add to it. They navigated the cluttered room without a single crash or bang, stepping over the wide shaft of light that flooded from behind the doorjamb, bisecting the darkness. No sound would betray their movements: vigilance was their master and they were its adroit pupils. They shut the door and stood, waiting, as their eyes adjusted to the darkness. Then they made for the intimate corner. The man went first and she followed, gripped by a fear the source of which she could not determine.

It was not their first time doing this.

"What's wrong?" the man whispered, treading cautiously through the debris.

"Nothing." She swallowed nervously. "But I'm afraid."

"Don't be afraid," he replied automatically, attempting to diffuse her uncertainty.

The light from the staircase had withered to an anemic trickle, oozing like blood and pooling in a wide puddle by the doorsill. He reached the corner, turned and saw her: a pair of eyeballs, phosphorescent like those of some nocturnal creature, glittering in the darkness.

"Don't be afraid," he repeated. "Come here."

She remained rigid, unmoving. He exhaled, attempting to soothe himself with the half-thought that time did not exist down here.

"Things will work out," his voice quavered, "as always. We've done pretty well so far, haven't we?"

"Yes."

"Okay, then. Come here!"

"But I'm scared!"

He reached out and took hold of her; she trembled, but otherwise did not resist. He reckoned that her behavior was little more than a sign of her ambivalence and that what he was about to do would dispel whatever bizarre fear it was that impelled it. He was not worried. In previous encounters, she had been even less disposed to make love, but he had succeeded in convincing her nonetheless and they had both succeeded in keeping the affair a secret.

He approached her neck and affixed his mouth to her flesh, cold and pulsing against his lips. He pulled her body onto his own, his lips migrating toward her chest. He felt his forehead graze the tight-fastened buttons of her dress, black and appropriately modest for the occasion. Upstairs, he remembered, the event was the culprit of this grievous attire and her attitude to match.

Women are such fragile, emotional spirits. He would have to persevere, he realized, if he was to alleviate this affliction of hers; this concern with what was happening above them – not an

22

unreasonable concern, but nonetheless irrelevant to his own desire. He shrugged off the remaining garments of his doubt, reassuring himself that his presence here, with her, was the greatest consolation he could offer.

He set his hands to the task of loosening the buttons of her dress. When he reached the last one which fastened the seam over her belly, he felt the flame of his desire leap from its brazier, setting his body alight. She took his hand and whispered into his ear, beseeching him:

"Slow down. Let us sit, first."

He detached himself reluctantly.

"I want to rest," she said. "I'm tired."

"Alright," he replied and knelt to prepare the ragged, disheveled bedding in the corner.

As he fiddled, the wet cloth released a familiar odor: the scent of last week's climax. He marveled at the savor a woman makes in a man's company, during her moment of pleasure. And he marveled at the way a woman, in the throes of her euphoria, releases her muffled shriek and, like a feline in heat, thrusts her claws deep into the lover's skin. He had taken immense pleasure, nearly identical to the tumbling swoon of his own orgasm, when she had done this to him during their last encounter. But this pleasure had been fleeting: his head clearing, his mood sobering, he heard her far-off voice say:

"Why did you cover my mouth? You were suffocating me!"

23

It was true. He had purposely muffled her pleasure, subduing her shriek, by placing a hand over her mouth. She had responded in kind, sinking her teeth into the flesh of his palm, like a wolf. But he bore the pain without much thought about it – he could not allow the other tenants in the building to know of their private scandal.

"Hey!" she said, drawing him out of his stupor. "Are you listening? Why did you cover my mouth with your hand?"

"Because your voice was scandalous."

"You made it scandalous," she replied.

"What do you mean?"

"Come on," she said, laughing, "don't be such a weasel."

He nodded in agreement, but could not look her in the eye. He pulled up his trousers and began buttoning his open shirt. He heard her say:

"It *will* be a scandal if we don't act quickly!"

Her breathing, he noticed, had returned to its usual, steady pace.

He shuddered, brought back to the present by the completion of his task. He glanced over at her: a form huddled into the corner of the darkened space. The look on her face was a question awaiting his response – not a rhetorical question, but the sort of question that was asked solely to comfort the asker and which had no real regard for the answer that could follow. Suddenly, he realized what it was that she was trying to do. *This will be our last time*, he thought to himself. *If I don't put an end to her insistence, she'll wear me forever – like a fetid shirt.*

But, his mind vacillated, *there's no harm in one last time*. He felt himself swept towards her, carried like flotsam on the tide of his own lust.

"My love," she said, "you must act quickly. They'll slaughter me if you don't!"

"Why are you in such a hurry?" he asked, gently attempting to put off the conversation she was now forcing upon him. "There's a time for everything."

"No," she yelled in his face, "the time is now! What's wrong with you? I told you, my period is already 10 days late!"

He squirmed.

"Those symptoms affect girls, occasionally. Don't worry. You'll get your period again."

She stared intently at his averted face, but he would not meet her gaze. She unhitched her tears, carrying forth:

"I'm not a *girl*," she replied. "You made me a woman. Did you forget?"

No, he had not forgotten. He had not forgotten his promise to take care of everything before the end of the month; had not forgotten his promise that his mother, somehow, would recover from her sudden illness; had not forgotten that he would be her lover for eternity and she would be his love until death. He wiped her tears. He pinched her cheek, then her waist, then her thigh. She moaned, muttering something – he could not tell what, but he knew what it meant: she was agreeing to one more time.

The bed in the corner was ready.

He sat down, reaching out to claw at her leg. Her knees, shaking, bent toward him. He grasped her violently, holding her face between his palms. She flexed and threw herself back from him, trying to assuage his passion, but he was undeterred. His fingers relinquished her face and moved on to her breasts, while his teeth nibbled, swiftly and consecutively, along the row of her lips. She groaned and nestled into him. He felt his blood smolder, bubbling up into his head, infecting him with a feverish madness. He could not keep his balance any longer.

In the moment of his climax, he ascertained that this would, indeed, be his last time with her. And in keeping with this ultimate encounter between lovers, he would have her – no, he *shall* have her – to his ultimate satisfaction. He shall take her over and over until, at her final yielding, she dissolves into his body – or perhaps he shall dissolve into hers. This shall be the last time and he should not abate a single thing. She belonged to him: this man who had made her a woman; a woman who, until his coming, was a naïve virgin, a mere girl, who could not possibly understand men. And in taking her, he had revealed to her the scent of her womanhood: that climactic savor which brought her into an awareness of her feminine self. *Yes,* he thought, *I should be free to shape her according to my wishes.*

26

He launched himself into her like a carnivorous beast, gnawing at his favorite parts of her, rending her clothes from her body without even giving her a chance to remove them. The sound of tearing fabric awakened within him something primal, lupine, ravenous. He drank in her musk, felt it pickle his mind, course through every length of his interstices, besotting him. Darkness encroached upon her blazing eyes; encroached upon the hulking silhouettes, the bodies, human and inanimate, scattered across the coarse cellar floor. The darkness merged with the wide skid of light oozing from behind the door, merged with the susurration of vermin scuttling somewhere beyond their field of vision, merged with the muffled clatter of someone's feet tramping up the stairs. The darkness seeped into her aching voice, the voice that urged him to calm himself, calm himself…

The broken darkness merged with the wide streak of light—

With their inverted visions, entwined—

With the taste of blood.

Blood, seeping between his teeth, coating his tongue, trickling down his throat, provoking further his cannibal's feast upon her tender, violated flesh. His teeth left grooves in her tired tenderness. His jaws, twisting and biting, coaxed the blood that welled forth from under her skin.

I am being eaten alive, she realized, *by this desperate, hysterical wolf of a man. No human being should tolerate this.*

"You're my love," her voice rose, imploring. "Don't do that!"

27

The wolf snuffled, but he did not withdraw.

"I'm your darling!" she cried. "I… No! *Don't!*"

He carried on without regard for her pain, growling as he brutalized her.

"I will," he bellowed. "I'll take all of you!" His voice rose like a foul stench from the carrion-pit of his soul: "You're *mine*, you *bitch!*"

In the corner, the makeshift bed creaked under jerking limbs, weighed down by the savage body atop them. Fingers sought their way into the air, sought out something to grasp, floundered. Finally, her fingers found their mark in the soft flesh of his heavy back. She thrust her nails into him with the entire force of her desperate scream. His back erupted into a river of molten fire.

The resistant fingers carried on their quest along the cold, coarse floor, colliding with many things: soft things, hard things; things oblong, things of uncertain utility. The blind fingers did not know what they were grabbing, nor how it was that they grabbed. The fingers knew not where they carried their coldly clutched weapon, nor how they hit their target. No: the fingers did not even know what act they were committing.

The woman woke up to find her left hand covering a bloodied mouth – a mouth whose final scream *she* had muffled. She gazed at the corpse lying on the bed next to her, aghast, repeating to herself:

'Your voice was scandalous!'

'Your voice was scandalous!'

Some time passed before she had calmed herself enough to realize that her right hand was mired inside the man's body. She checked 10 times to make sure and it was true: her hand had sunk into his flesh, stabbing the man with some hard, unknown object which had since buried its identity inside him. It was only then that she remembered everything and the memory made her distressed. But then she stopped, remembering what he had called her.

She stared at the ceiling above her where, just like the cellar, a body was enclosed in a locked chamber.

"You," she said, "are the son of a bitch!"

THE LOCKED ROOM
[*Secrets of the Hourglass*, Chapter 2]
Elias Farkouh

As a body in hypnosis is led away from itself, so was she guided through the block of women who sat in the hallway. She hobbled into the kitchen and disappeared. An odd sense of levity was ravaging her. Or perhaps it was the opposite: she was strapped with some unholy weight that pulled her downward, deep into the pit of her fear. Women out in the hallway, their banter was reduced to quick susurrations, faintest ripples, so faint but ceaseless too; and that was their deadly besieging quality, the way they swirled gently and unimpeded about her head. They pounced on her all at once. Their shadows pooling at her feet and then ascending, coursing up her black dress like a battalion over a rampart, encircling hips and thighs and navel; and then tightening, tightening, until the gates burst open and her citadel was overrun. A flower of pure horror bloomed within her. A sudden shiver passed over her. She blinked.

Now she saw everything.

She understood it all: every movement, every sound.

There, inside the locked room, a daring sort of motion; shameless even. Someone uttered an expectorant hiss in accompaniment. She shook her head as though she were in need of sobering up. But no, her surroundings were real, she was not dreaming – hypnotized maybe, but awake. That mortuary block of women in funereal shrouds kowtowing towards the center, rising up again,

31

repeating. She watched from the kitchen, her thoughts crackling like radio static over the stubborn beat of her heart. The women were talking with their mouths full, rude morsels of half-masticated gossip stuck to their mouths, winking with open eyes over rumor and scandal, secrets stripped of their secrecy.

She was still the only one who saw it. None of them did – she was certain of it. She had glimpsed that swift, subtle movement there, across the hall in the locked room. There was no mistaking it. The woman performed it as though she was embarking upon a pilgrimage of her own perversion.

She was the only one who had heard it: the voice of a demon conjured from the throat of a willing host; its vile resonance oozing paper-thin from under the locked door of the room.

The locked room.

Over there,
    or rather,
        over here.

              A few more steps until the door. A few steps, but with heavy legs, to the wooden door – that was all it was, but it blocked the view, muffled the sound. It was to this door that one woman gestured, shouting at her over her pointed chin:

"Shut it!"

And so she did.

She could not understand how it was that this woman's power had crept in and penetrated her. She could not know how she had been made a hostage of those piercing eyes, scarab-blue. And yet, she still found herself subject to their authority: the quick, darting movements, flashing and glimmering, unvoiced but entirely readable. In this locked room where everything took place in a stately silence, a weirdly pagan sanctity that gushed forth from everything like a bottomless aquifer, her voice was useless. Everything here submitted unto death, present in the naked body recumbent upon the whiteness of the bed, trembling amid the awful movement surrounding it.

As if the woman was rubbing at the spot on her neck from which the flower of life was supposed to spring forth. She rubbed at this spot again and again, calm and assiduous, fondling it gently, summoning it in a mystical language. But the flower did not rise. She smiled, her forgiveness transparent, running down her face, and she went back to her rubbing and prodding – unoccupied, but with the act of rubbing alone, indifferent to the vivacity and the noise of existence outside,

beyond the door,

inside the house wallowing in the despair of its present death,

and the women dressed in black who were congregating here to begin the body's final bath, tonight.

She heard her say, in a voice not wanting to ascribe itself to the sanctity of the place:

"Bring me some fresh water."

She edged toward the bed, its frame tremulous over the naked body whose violated flesh jostled beneath the rubbing and the praying. She stood a few feet away, examining the mysterious vibrations which possessed her as she bent over the whitened body, the locks of black hair, the bare shoulders notched by the omnipresent weight of a brassiere; the relaxed legs slumped over the edge of the bed, toenails speckled with crusted pink polish jutting rudely into the air.

The voice beckoned, quietly but firmly:

"Come closer."

She moved toward the bed, but apparently she was not fast enough and the older woman clamped a hand on her wrist, pulling her in. The grip of the woman hurt and she attempted to groan, but the silent room kept her voice from escaping. The eyes of the woman, the color of blood, bored into her, unsoftened by the compliance she was attempting to affect. Her throat seemed to her as if it were overgrown with some obstinate briar and she swallowed painfully, closing her eyes. The image of a whitened body, abject in its nakedness, flickered weirdly against the insides of her eyelids. The woman grasped her hand, using her fingers to prod the corpse as though she were some manner of medical instrument.

She felt the lifelessness of the body, an eerie ductility beneath her fingers, and now she really saw it, gazing with dismay upon the cold, pliant breast as it responded like a wad of dough to her touch. The breath of the other woman, hot and volcanic, stole over her face as she hissed, inviting her to conspiracy:

"Do you see?…Do you *see?*"

When she gave no answer – she could not believe she was actually hearing the concealed invitation of this woman – her interlocutor drew herself even closer to her face, pressing her wrist with the grip of a man.

"Do you also have this beauty," she asked, "—*in here?*"

"What?"

The word came out harsh and rattling as though she were being strangled to death. Before she could protest, the woman thrust two powerful fingers beneath the black cloth of her shirt.

"This," she said, prodding her breast.

Under the pressure of the woman's touch, she felt her heart dislodge from its station and plunge down the open fissure inside her.

"Bring me some fresh water," the woman said.

She turned back to the cadaver, resuming her intimate discourse with the flower of life, so elusive. She summoned it, searched and prodded the length of the whitened corpse, bathing it in the awful tepid water; the cresting soap bubbles amassing whirlpool-style in the dead, recessed hide of the navel.

She obeyed and left the room. The commanding female took no notice of the horror branded on her face, her eyes shooting lasers into the corpse as she kneaded and washed… took no notice of the single tear that manifested at the edge of one eye, obscuring the source of her horror.

Time shattered, disemboweled. She saw the steaming mass of its ejected interstices, memories piled to the sky like so many corpses,

and revealed before her was a boundless, stygian wilderness where hissing conspirators and prodding digits roamed,

but where Madness ruled as supreme master (he had long been expelled from Hell, too volatile for the rest of the demons),

unmasking taboos in every utterance and every bare movement; stealing into locked rooms and enslaving the occupants in his doomed, unflagging search (he was Madness, after all) for the black flower of life: that mythical plant whose only known matrix was the ruined flesh of the dead.

In shattered time, her own living body swayed to the convulsive wicked pleasure and she was overcome with terror as it snagged like a mat of insidious algae on the curled ends of her hair, awakening her blood, prodding her flesh with the forceful maleness of its grip. Her body numbed, her vision clouded... Her boiling blood sent up a column of steam, obscuring her thoughts – anticipation for a pleasure that she could never indulge. She felt her violated breast throbbing, the stillborn trembling inside her belly: an insidious passenger whose hunger she knew she would never sate.

She leaned against the kitchen wall, her senses adrift,

and the requested water was boiling,

and her blood boiled, too; and she felt herself steeped in a compulsion to return to the locked room, to challenge the manlike fingers of the woman, gripping them back with this new, queer pleasure; those hands which she knew could satisfy her more than the defeated murmur of a man.

That mighty, hulking woman – could she read the pain etched in the corners of the lifeless, downturned mouth? With what manner of instruments would she analyze the dry, barren soil of the dead woman's garden, unwatered by a man for how many years? Could she feel the pliant response of the tissue, the static, unheaving chest, as she kneaded and provoked it, taming and relaxing it, edging the flesh toward defeat? Had she drawn the constellatory line between these two yawning deprivations: the one that moldered in her mother's dead body and the one that had assumed control of her own living flesh, awake and ready to receive those prodding fingers that searched for a black-blooming prize?

And what kind of life was it that fed such a blossom?

A black one, of course.

Over the past 10 years, maybe longer, her mother's fields had gone fallow, wasted without the care of a man. When her final caregiver died, he was survived by four varieties of cacti:

One on top of his tomb; and her promiscuous brother who was absent now from this place: she had seen him sneak out the door that night, following the neighbor-girl down into the basement like an overgrown puppy. An eager beaver – eager to fornicate in the clandestine darkness below. She watched her brother signal clumsily to the girl, *Go down the stairs ahead of me, I'll catch up.* Such a brat, her brother, being the man he was: he would play with her, then dispose of her when it was time. She thought she might like to warn her, but her conscience, that frothing river of blood that coursed through the darkened wilderness of her body, told her *No, leave them be* – and it was out of her hands.

And her mother – just 10 years a married woman. She was 19 when they sang to her, dressing her in white. She dreamed of everlasting happiness and many children. The reality of her marriage was disappointing. The groom, who became the husband, who became the father: he was neither responsible nor loving.

He sowed two seeds in his wife during their first few years of marriage, but that was all. He scattered the remainder of his store in other fields. They lived together for 10 years and then the desolation of her mother began. She was 29. She became, for all men with lusty eyes, a pendulous cluster of grapes just asking to be picked and devoured; a lewd, scavenging fantasy that left her bound and writhing over the cooking fire of a marauder. Their eyes said it, their faces and mouths, said it all fluently in mute language, that the same type of bullets fired at her wedding 10 years ago… 13 years ago… 17 years ago… might end her life one day – that is, *if* there was no man to protect her. Yes, she understood the lesson being dictated to her. She had roughened a little over the years, but she was by no means unsexable. She married again as fast as she could – while she still could.

"My word," someone said at the second wedding. "She's so succulent – like a peach!"

The man's eyes licked hungrily at her mother in the wedding gown.

"She's my *mother*," she hissed in response.

And the man nodded without taking his gaze off the dais.

"Look at this belly! It belongs to a girl in her 20s," hissed the woman who bent over her mother's body, scrubbing and wheedling.

She was scrubbing the shaded region underneath the heavy breasts. With a soft sponge held open-palmed, she passed over the sides of the corpse, touched the neck with her fingertips, meandered her way slowly to the breasts, groping and pressing them together like someone bent to drink water from a stream, her face an inch from the dead flesh. She paused and released a low animal growl, sliding her bare arms forcefully toward the dented belly, all the way to the pelvis. She remained there as if taken by a sudden fatigue or stupor.

"Change the water!" the woman hissed.

She met her gaze and blanched: two embers out of deepest Hell. And the young woman was the fourth of her father's cacti:

She was, for so long, the bedridden wife of a man born to lose. And she was doomed to witness his defeat over and over: the arid whinny, the rainless thunderclap, the aimless crescendo bereft of

39

its climax, the self-consuming burn of contact; skin-on-skin friction that fed itself, the blood circulating endlessly inside his closed-off veins, the useless beads of sweat that formed of their own accord on her skin, like an insult, for even the coldest water could not quench the terrible, unyielding heat of her body. Years passed. The young tigress became ever more wrathful, brutal; untamed by the saccharine nonsense of her husband and his fumbling, dry caresses. Her man knew that he did not please her. His eyes fumbled for hers, then, out of shame, averted their intended course. He could not weaken the slow, resolute power of her urges: he visualized his sex as a shallow breaker over which the tidal swell of his wife's desire simply rolled inland, unbreaking, toward a more worthy obstacle. Any obstacle: it did not matter.

The corpse stretched out recumbent beneath the woman's prodding fingers, bespeaking its own defeat. She studied the corpse and decided that it was acknowledging, on the one hand, not only defeat, but also, on the other hand, the wily substitute, The Next Step. The corpse had taken it for granted, but she had not until now: now the idea was taking over; now it was pulling her tiger-mind into its folds. The Next Step. Yes.

The numbness spread to the pit of her belly and her mind wandered, first to the fever that had made the corpse burn bright and quick and then extinguish, its life-fuel all spent, to the funerary block of women who sat in the hallway. She paid them no mind as she passed, holding the bucket of hot water in her feverish hands. The water sloshed and stung her skin, but she did not mind: she had long been familiar with a different kind of sting, more deeply felt. That pain etched itself like graffiti on the inner wall of her barrenness, raking its red-hot fingernails through her as though it was bound up and trying to escape. That pain, set into renewed motion by the feeling of the hand of the older on her breast – that lively, robust, youthful breast; prepared, provoked and protruding, or rather intruding, through the half-cracked door.

"Shut it," the older woman said.

She shut it. She did not need to be told to shut it. She shut the door because she wanted to. Because she knew that what was about to happen required a closed door, perhaps even a locked door.

She had seen herself performing this action long before she was required to, standing in the kitchen to refill the ablutatory bucket. She knew the role that she was meant to perform and she rehearsed it silently to herself over the welling progression of the bucket filling up, shutting off the spigot and turning, first her mind and then her feet, in the direction of the locked room. She shuffled down the hallway, water sloshing, as though she were compelled by some greater force outside of time and choice and truth or falsity: an oracle bound up and made wholly participant in the fulfillment of her final prophecy.

She entered the room and shut the door. She shut it because she knew that the matter at hand could occur only behind a closed door,

     inside a locked room,

       between two creatures of equal design,

And a third, unmoving and ceraceous, splayed out in its casual, submitting nudity to the barrage of prodding fingers.

She reached the bed and halted. The mighty, barren woman did not look up: she was still absorbed in her search for the flower of life. Soapy water sloshed from a bucket, running down into the spread-legged crevasse of the weighted mattress. Sweat dripped from a featureless face onto busy, viselike hands. Dead and live odors mixed and swirled, filling the locked room with a perfume of profanity.

"Put it down," the mighty woman said, gesturing to the bucket.

She set it down, locking eyes with the other woman.

"She's dead," she uttered, softly.

The other woman did not respond. She knelt over the corpse, her hands frozen upon the spot that she had been working. The younger woman moved in closer, reached out and touched her bent back. Her fingers passed gently over its contours, navigating the curvature of the spine. The mighty woman stood without turning to face her. The exploring hand rested for a moment on her shoulder: not the grip of a man, but the grip of a woman.

"She's *dead*," she said again, more emphatic this time.

And she worked her body in closer to the other woman, inviting her to the inevitable act.

"Look here," she said.

She spoke with utter solemnity, a quiet confidence. The elder woman turned and finally met her gaze. She could see the frenzy building inside her, the hulking body electric with desire, impelled by an inner dynamo set off by the squeeze of a breast, the prod of an instrument any human touch, as though her mordant skin were inlaid with a grid of buried sensors, a minefield of stimulus-and-response.

"Here!"

Trembling fingers unfastening the black shirt,

"Here!"

The voice repeating, quickening,

"Here!"

Naked to the waist, she took the mighty woman's hand and planted it on one ponderous bosom exposed to the perfumed air. At first, the alien hand resisted, exhibiting a strange sort of inertia, resting heavily beneath her pulsing throat, until the other woman moved even closer, panting sweatily,

"It's alive. It's strong. Feel it! Don't be afraid; grab it, touch it." And braying like a draft horse, "it's *alive!*"

And she dared, merging into the only other *she* on earth,

at the edge of a trembling bed,

under mute surveillance by a waxen body,

behind a closed door,

in a locked room,

where the black rook of Death circled slowly, beating a silent
dirge for a flower that did not exist.

THE BRASS KOHL POT
Basma el-Nsour

The approach of the young man caught me off guard. I tried, perhaps too hard, to conceal my abashment when he said:

"Excuse me – you're sitting in my seat."

To be perfectly honest, I had no idea that my ticket came with an assigned seat. I fumbled for an apology, overwhelmed with embarrassment, and made to leave. But now the young man, who was also showing some uneasiness about the whole situation, offered to leave his seat in exchange for mine. A kind gesture, but of course I refused. I would not say so, but I thought it best that a man like this, so genial and accommodating, deserved this seat above all others, since the one next to it was occupied by a beautiful young lady. It was a long journey ahead and in that time they could come to know one another, perhaps become friends or even lovers. Who knows? I imagined the two of them ending up in a happy marriage: the kind in which they would reflect contentedly, from time to time, on the circumstances which brought them together – a story which, in their telling, would see me playing my part over and over again, humbly and namelessly, but always assigned the proper degree of gratitude.

The man, truly a gentleman, helped me to find my seat. I spent a long moment struggling through the contents of my purse, rummaging about until I found my ticket at the very bottom. At that moment, a bottle of pills tumbled out of my purse, sending its contents clattering over the bus floor. Both of us dropped to our knees in an effort to recover what had been spilled. Offering me a cupped handful of pills, the man asked sympathetically:

"I hope it's nothing serious?"

I shook my head.

"Just a migraine that attacks me now and then."

I found my seat – the one printed on the ticket – and sat down. The spot next to me was empty, which made me feel a little disappointed. I thought I should try to relax, but it was not meant to be: passengers kept boarding the bus, jostling and crowding through the aisle. I decided that I would spy on them, just to pass the time – innocent fun, really; just an aimless little game I would resort to whenever I felt lonely.

Just a few minutes before the bus was scheduled to depart, the last passenger boarded. He was a somber-looking man, the kind whose expression of sullen disgust seemed so practiced as to be effortless, maybe even permanent. Without so much as a word, he threw his body brusquely into the seat next to mine – I barely had time to snatch up my purse before he sat on it! It was clear to me that this man had no idea how to treat a lady, so I ignored him as best I could. Which is to say I fidgeted in distress, checked my watch, dropped my purse between my feet, then picked it up again, settled it in my lap and proceeded to sift aimlessly through its contents. All the while, my neighbor's countenance expressed the deepest resentment. I tried to sit still.

I studied the road for a time and then closed my eyes, remembering the sad face that had, in its own circuitous way, launched my foolish heart on this journey.

"Your eyes are amazingly beautiful," he had said in a voice that reflected some sort of defeat as it uttered those words – the words that installed themselves in the forefront of my memory for a whole year: "Your eyes are amazingly beautiful."

I think I smiled, right then, recalling his words.

My scowling seatmate, who must have noticed the change in my expression, shifted his eyes toward me in sudden bewilderment. I needed no more invitation than this.

"Just me on this trip," I blurted. "No company to speak of! A woman travelling alone – can you imagine that? I bought the ticket myself. Then I had to deal with, you know, a rather tasteless incident before I found this seat: dropped my medicine bottle, you see; pills everywhere. But," I said, regaining my composure, "other than that, everything went smoothly."

The man shot me a glance of pure disdain, then pulled a newspaper from his pocket. I resumed my cross-examination:

"Is this your first trip to Aqaba?"

"Been working there for years," he said, his eyes boring into the paper before him. "I take this trip twice a week."

My eyes widened.

"Lucky you!" I said.

He offered a smile entirely devoid of goodwill – as if to say, *There is nothing lucky about this interaction* – and went back to his newspaper. I pondered the street and its occupants, watching them recede from view as the bus rumbled onward. I took off my glasses and proceeded to clean them carefully, meditatively, with a tissue.

Last year, I had taken this same journey with my brother and his family. He had assured me repeatedly that I would not be a wet blanket, despite the look his wife had given me (one of serious contempt). In the end, I had decided that I could not go against the wishes of my brother – even though, strictly speaking, I am several years his elder.

When I was young, my brother was such a naughty child. He would— Oh, wait a minute, now— Damn it, did I forget to mention my age? Sorry, this is a bad habit of mine. Let us just say that I have crossed the 40-yard-line in my years. In fact, I am really closer to 50 these days and no, I still have not found myself a husband. Let me put this as simply as I can: I am a spinster.

While we are being frank with each other, let me also say that I *loathe* this word, 'spinster.' It has this macabre quality to it, at once reductive and profound, that smacks of the most depressing sort of fatalism; the kind one might reserve for an incurable disease or a state of permanent disability.

In my defense – for, you see, I cannot help but defend myself against such an ugly word – I am a very pleasant spinster, certainly a burden to no one but myself. I have had a successful career.

Okay… I should not say 'successful,' as I have no achievements worth mentioning here, but I am a remarkably fast typist. And I am not boring: I enjoy reading poetry and romance novels. Hell, I even fell in love once – when was that? I cannot recall precisely, but I want to say it was maybe 20 years ago… Damn it all! I have let my mind wander once again. Let us return to our story:

As soon as we had installed ourselves in our hotel, my brother, my sister-in-law and the children all went tramping down to the beach. I had announced that I wanted to explore the city, but no one was interested in accompanying me, so I went out alone.

After a while, I found an eastern antiques shop and wandered in. Some soft, mellow tune was emanating from an indeterminate spot in a darkened corner of the room. As my eyes adjusted to the light, I realized that there was a man sitting there, half-hidden in the shadows. He stood up, welcomed me with a smile and asked if I was looking for anything in particular. I looked around, somewhat confounded – the place was full to bursting with antiques – before my eyes fell on a brass kohl pot covered with dust. I pointed at it eagerly.

"That's what I'm looking for!"

"I'm sorry," he said with a smile, "but that one isn't for sale. I'm holding it for personal reasons. How about something else?"

"Actually," I said, "I don't want anything else. This kohl pot is the one for me."

He shook his head lovingly.

"You don't need it. Your eyes are amazingly beautiful."

No one had ever said anything like that to me before.

I choked on some inchoate word, found I actually had nothing to say, smiled awkwardly and left the shop. That statement of his persisted in my memory from that moment onward, cropping up uninvited at the most bizarre moments to sit beside me in my daydreams, distracting my mind with its caresses, so that the sound of my typing became somehow fuller, more compassionate. It was that single, compassionate utterance that compelled me to visit Aqaba once more: a visit that has not cost me anything other than a bus ticket, a day off from work and a white lie to get my boss to agree to it.

I sighed, glanced at my watch, fiddled with my purse. My sour-faced neighbor gave me a look of protest, to which I responded with a rueful smile: it seemed that I had gone back to fidgeting. Oh, well.

I looked over at the young man whose seat I had taken. His pretty, young neighbor and himself were absorbed in a hushed conversation, almost whispering; the kind of conversation that requires intimate physical proximity. I surveyed the rest of the passengers: most were pale in the face, probably from hunger or the claustrophobic privation of a journey by bus. We were nearing our destination. The sea, through the window, was obscenely blue. The bus came to a halt and the passengers began to file out into the sunlight. The young man and young woman waved to me as they left, disappearing together into the tangled streets.

I found myself, alone, in the center of the city. My sulky travel companion had vanished. I hitched up my purse and set it firmly on my shoulder, trying to ignore my hunger. My legs were a bit shaky from the journey, but I pulled myself together and set about locating the street where my shop was located. When I finally found it, I stood outside for a while, reading the sign over and over and taking short, measured breaths. I opened the door cautiously: door chimes rang out like church bells. I was quite certain those were not here last year.

Across the shop, a young man was standing behind the glass counter, chatting with a blonde customer about a carved wooden camel of which she was clearly enamored. I guessed that the young man must be the assistant to my shopkeeper. I approached the counter taking slow, deliberate steps, but the assistant paid me no regard. The blonde customer left the shop with a camel-shaped package in tow. Meanwhile, the young man went about rearranging the items he had taken out to show to the tourist, while the shopkeeper stood beside the counter working on what appeared to be a watch. I studied his face: he had not changed a bit. He lifted his head suddenly and I saw his cheerless eyes in full, crystalline relief. He was aware of my presence.

"Don't you see," he said, rebuking his assistant harshly, "that we've got a customer waiting? Help this lady here, then finish whatever you're doing."

He lowered his eyes and resumed his work. The young man walked around the counter and came over to me, adopting a faint smile and an air of mock tenderness as he said:

"What can I do for you?"

I looked around, somewhat confounded – the place was full to bursting with antiques – but I could not find the brass kohl pot. I gave the shopkeeper one final glance before I turned to leave, and said, with some difficulty:

"Nothing. Nothing at all."

THE OLD MAN AND THE SNOW
Ahmed Abu Hleiwa

I. The Old Man and the Snow

For wayfarers who pass through these parts in winter, the only indication of human life in the mountain villages is the smoke escaping from chimneys: a bare scrap of life among the encompassing death that the seasons impose. The clouds devour the warmth of the sun, the cold immobilizes everyone; the land, like a corpse, is shrouded in snow.

He had left his home in the morning. How chilly a winter morning on a mountain!

He was old now: an old man who had spent many of his latter years in a state of grief and yearning. He had lost his wife long ago and his sons too had left him: packed up and moved to the city where they lived now, he imagined, in a constant bid for sustenance — a sustenance that was unmistakably urban, tinged with noise and hustle.

His tenuous steps carried him along the same old path, which resolved each year in the same place: the grave of his wife. Without giving it too much thought, he had made a custom of visiting her grave each year in the middle of January, on the anniversary of her death, usually accompanied by his youngest son. This year, however, he walked the path alone. Like all of his sons when they had reached a certain age, his youngest had fled the mountain village as if it were on fire, dreaming of the city and the beautiful women who, no doubt, awaited him there.

The graveyard where his wife was interred sat on a precipice overlooking the village. A chilly wind tore through the place; the old cypress trees, bent like beggars beneath sacks of snow, groaned, swaying precariously. Down below, the old man – back hunched, cane creaking, white-haired and snow-dusted – looked like some creature conjured from the ice: a golem shuffling slowly over the frozen ground.

At last, the old man reached the graveyard. With footfalls bitten by frost and weakened by the fatigue of his ascent, he navigated his way through the quiet rows of headstones. The cold penetrated his body; the cold gnawed at his bones. There it was: the grave of his wife. He greeted her and mumbled *Al-Fatiha* to her departed soul. His lips trembled, his tongue was a deathbed for the words. His strength gave out and he collapsed in a heap upon her grave. Hot tears sprang from behind his eyes; a strangled, arrhythmic pulse belied his long-broken heart. Sobbing, the old man recounted everything to her: what a wreck he had become, what a miserable thing life had become, in the time since her departure.

The cold was tightening its grip on his body. He tried to get up – his breath quickened as his legs, barely respondent, failed beneath him. His cane, too, proved useless. He felt as though his whole body was betraying him. He tried again to stand, this time falling prone atop the grave of his wife; his face buried in the snow, his face burning with tears. He heard his wife calling him:

Adam, you must rest, my Adam. Come closer. Closer, now. Closer…

He lay there splayed out upon the grave, a creature divided. His left hand plunged deep into the snow, while his right hand grasped impotently at the pathetic cane. His wife called him again:

Time for you to rest, Adam. Come closer to me: Closer... Closer.

That final word, "Closer," rang out like a bell within the soul of the old man, drowning out all other stimuli, all memories, so that he felt a strange sort of warmth undiminished by the coldness of nature, the coldness of old age, the coldness of children who no longer needed their parents. He let go of the cane and buried both of his hands in the snow, repeating the word, *Closer*, skillfully and with certainty.

Night fell and then other nights fell and the snow-laden January drifted away on the wind. In another year, it would come back, dragging with it the chariots of Winter – but it would be alone next time, without the old man and without the snow.

II. One Body's Transit

The city swept up the refuse of its nightly debauchery, covering its nudity with the chaste garments of dawn. The city roused its sleepers, scattered the dark dreams of lovers, with the morning light. A new day began, a new misadventure: houses sweated silently in their boredom, sighs puffed like smoke from lungs strained and stressed; despair, salty and viscous, trickled steadily from ancient, irreparable sores. Poverty hung about the heads of the destitute like clouds of exhaust: it was the air they breathed unto death. Custom robbed us of our last emotion. Tradition – that unwritten, unspoken martial law – snuffled like a dog at the burned-out corpse of our humanity. That was life in the city: a fresh slice of Hell.

The roof: on its precipice stood the belle, arms outstretched, her body cruciform in the space between Heaven and Earth. She surveyed the muddled skyline of the city, allowing her gaze to wander off into the horizon. Her mind dredged up a jarring selection of memories – some from a distant, beautiful past, while others invoked her present reality in all its grotesque immediacy. The crowd below was beginning to augment itself like a swarm of insects: multifarious, but at the same time single-minded – whispering, chattering, shouting, holding their breaths, staring.

She jumped.

From the fourth floor, a man interpreted the body's transit:

What cowardice, this criminal! Her answer to life was suicide!

From the third floor, a woman issued her own interpretation:

What courage, this poor victim! Her answer to life was suicide!

From the second floor, a little boy:

Why would she do that?

From the first floor, a little girl:

But… Why?

Out on the street, the body made impact, splattering the crowd and the buildings and the cars with a steaming red liquid. On the pavement, the body collapsed into a mound of barely distinguishable parts of flesh, bone, teeth, hair, sinew. Then it shrunk until it was no more – the liquid soaked into the ground, the color faded from the clothes of the people, evaporated off the cars and the sidewalk. The steam fused with the sky, became part of the clouds, and faded away. With nothing left to do, the crowd dispersed, each of them free to flutter inside a cage of their own daily banalities.

THE BACKYARD
Magdalene Abu el-Rub

She walked into the lightless backyard, searching carefully and assiduously for a place to set herself down in the dark. The coldness of the night-moistened ground crept upward through the soles of her feet, diluting her bodily warmth. The twin rain tanks of the building stood, lurking in the darkness against the courtyard wall, like sentinels guarding an ancient temple. She approached and sat down on a rock in the space between them. The tanks emitted a strong odor of mildew, which took her off guard. She hunched over in a posture of tortured contemplation, her legs bent and hugged to her chest, her chin nestled atop them. She did not know for how long she would have to sit there, but given the alternative she knew that she could probably last until daybreak at least, maybe longer.

She had slunk away from the apartment, her face stained with tears, feeling equanimity eaten away by dread: the relentless pain and secret, rumbling anger which made up her everyday life. She only wanted to leave. Time did not factor into this equation. She wanted to leave forever, wanted them to feel the shame they deserved for their awful treatment of her. *Once I'm gone*, she thought, *perhaps they'll realize how much they cared for me.* She stole quietly out the back, thinking of before, when

It is almost midnight and one of her brothers is shouting to her:

"Girl! Where'd you go? Make us a pot of tea!"

When she enters the room with the teapot on its tray, she is invisible: her brothers are sitting in a circle around the card table, laughing and bullshitting, ribbing and kicking. She sets the tray beside them and goes back to her room, where she sits alone, looking out onto the backyard.

There was a time not so long ago when she had known her own backyard only as one sees it from a window: a few anemic cypresses lined against the moldering fence, a ragged tribe of water tanks in varying stages of weather-beaten neglect; the ground covered in trash, carried in by the wind or deposited more willfully by the tenants; bits of fabric that had once hung proudly on the clothesline of some neighbor until the wind stole them away and fashioned them into a series of cruel, vexillographic puns.

She is looking down on the backyard from above, thinking about running away. It is the view from her window that puts her in this mood. She knows that when she makes her exodus, the backyard will be her staging-ground. Her point of no return.

A sudden cacophony emanates from the room downstairs. Voices raised, guffaws, howls and hoots. The voice of Marwan voice is the loudest just as his hands are the dirtiest. These are merely the *accoutrements* of his trade as an auto-mechanic. His grease-blackened hands have left stains in nearly every towel in the house.

She prods her bruised shoulder tenderly, examines the bluing welts on her legs with a sense of detachment. These stains are also the doing of Marwan. The other night he had planted a kick in her back − *her back!* − while she lay on the floor, unable to defend herself from the blows he had rained upon her head and face. When it was clear that the anger of Marwan had passed, her mother 'stepped in' (having watched the whole episode without uttering so much as a word of protest) and said:

"That's enough, Marwan, let her go. I'll have my own 'conversation' with her later."

The cold and damp air, the lonely frigidness of her stone perch wedged between the ghostly rain-barrel sentinels, made her shiver. She blinked as her eyes grew accustomed to the dim, the hulking shadow of her apartment building shading slowly into relief against the strange undark of the urban night. She stared up into the windows, mostly dark, including her own.

Here was one lighted window on the first floor, half-curtained, where a newlywed couple was living. They had moved in on the day of their wedding, accompanied by the entire ridiculous nuptial train of family members and friends, singers and drummers, whose inescapable noise echoed and rumbled through every corner of the building.

Another lighted window, a place occupied by a lady who might have become her mother-in-law had happier scenarios prevailed. This lady appeared one day at the very doorstep of her family to inquire whether they might be able to furnish her son with a wife. And as she was leaving, she had whispered to the girl's mother,

"Your daughter is flawless, really. If only her skin was a little lighter – then we'd have a match!"

As she is stealing out of her room to make her escape, she takes care to tread lightly past her mother's door. She passes the rooms of her brothers with less caution for they are all busy with their card game. Next, she passes the living room: her father is at his post on the couch facing the television, snoring loudly. Her father has a strict policy of 'watching' only news programming – no fluff.

The television says:

"—that over the past week, the number of casualties has declined steadily, down from previous estimates of 60 deaths per day. The streets of Baghdad..."

She grasps and turns the doorknob with surgical caution, opening and shutting the door behind her, without so much as a clink or creak. She pads quietly down the darkened stairwell, her unease mounting with every step. She passes the threshold of the matchmaking lady on the first floor and her heart flutters a little, remembering the incident two days ago: her brother, Mahmoud, home from college for the weekend, had caught her lingering in front of this apartment. His first impulse was to slap her across the face. Then he ran upstairs to tell their mother.

In the backyard, on her rock between sentinels, she flinched. A cat sprang from the sedge by the fence, chased in turn by another cat. She drew her limbs in reflexively, banging her bruised shoulder against the rain barrel. She sobbed for as long as she felt like sobbing – a long time – and thought to herself:

I am prepared to tolerate much from my family, but when they beat me like this, they step over a line that can't be uncrossed.

62

Was it only three years ago that Mother fell ill? Has it been only three years that I've acted, in her stead, as this family's housekeeper?

Of course it was only the natural choice — I had suddenly become the only unmaimed female in the house. Who else would take care of them all?

Mother used to say of me:

"This girl is my youngest and my last. I always thought of her as something extra, a spare part kept on hand in case of emergency. And now look, how gracious is God! He gave us this child so that my infirmity doesn't destabilize this family."

Mother also said of me:

"So she has two years left in high school, big deal. It's not like she's any kind of prodigy. I say let her stay home."

Mother also said of me:

"God gave me two girls and three boys. This other one, I don't know where she came from, maybe the angels got mixed up. She even looks different. Where'd she get that tan, those thick eyebrows? Not this side of the family, I can tell you that!"

My two sisters, both of whom are married, tried once to pluck my eyebrows for me. But Mother got wind of it and put a stop to the whole thing. My sisters said that I had become a grown woman and it was time for me to start taking proper care of myself. But Mother yelled:

"Don't you dare say that in front of her! Womanhood is the last thing she needs to worry about right now. Just leave it alone. Even black hens lay white eggs."

I didn't know what Mother was talking about. Who's the black hen? Who or what is the white egg? I don't know.

How can Mother dismiss my potential as a student? Mahmoud is dumber than a sack of bricks and yet he's the one who gets to go off to college. I think all he's learned so far is how to brag at length about being in college. And, apparently, how to beat me up. Mahmoud, you bastard… You were the one who caught me outside the neighbor's place, handing a piece of paper to Samir, the young pharmacy attendant who lives there. You started beating me right there in the hallway. You didn't even ask me what I was doing and I didn't even have a chance to tell you, to say that the paper I gave Samir had nothing on it but the name of a skin-bleaching ointment I'd seen in a magazine.

Mahmoud marched me into the living room where I was to receive my sentence. Father was engrossed in his TV news. Mother, meanwhile, was going mad:

"Just wait until I sic Marwan and Majid on you. Maybe, then you'll learn a lesson!"

Then Mother turned the dogs loose. They beat me good and hard and locked me up in the house. I wasn't even permitted to take out the garbage.

For once, Mother was right: I really did learn my lesson. Ever since that beating, I've been suffocating. Something has been smoldering inside my lungs, but the smoke never escapes.

Majid beat me until his knuckles were raw. I could have outed him, but I didn't. I kept to myself the knowledge of what I'd found under his pillow. It

64

could have been my secret weapon. Instead, I found myself shredding the photos into tiny pieces and hiding them in the bottom of the wastebasket.

Her bare feet began to tremble against the freezing, sodden ground. She flinched again as the pair of sparring cats reappeared out of the darkness, yowling like Hades as they scrambled through the brush.

Only one window remained lit now, sending a dim shaft of light out onto the yard where she sat: a single beacon of familiarity on the outskirts of a vast unknown. Its light consoled her somewhat, but it did not dispel her fears.

What if a burglar is lurking somewhere around here, hidden in the shadows? This neighborhood has its fair share of burglaries.

What if some manner of venomous creature, scorpion-spider-snake, is scuttling over me right now, readying its fangs to strike?

What if anything at all were to happen right now? Where would I go? What would my family do to me, knowing that I tried to run away?

As this final thought crossed her mind, the light went off in the window across the way. Now she was all alone in the darkness, flanked by two ghostly barrels and monitored by two sets of glowing feline eyes. She eased herself down from her perch with great caution: she did not want a burglar to notice her or a scorpion to strike at her. All she wanted, right now, was the warm sanctuary of her room.

She climbed the darkened stairwell fearfully, listening carefully at the door of the apartment for any signs of life. No TV; no Father snoring. Everyone was sleeping, even her night-owl brothers. She breathed a sigh of relief. No one would know that she had gone out; tonight would be her little secret.

She turned the doorknob and pushed. The bolt jerked against the latch.

They had locked her out.

TATTOO
Asmaa al-Mallah

I. Demise

The palm of his hand is hemorrhaging blood. The only witness to this injury is a brittle-looking man standing apace away. Splintered glass lies about everywhere, casting reflected images of other parts of the room, of himself and the brittle man, at odd angles throughout his field of vision. Somehow, it makes him feel that the accident preceding it has punctured the space-time architecture of the universe.

It is a very strange situation. The details are vaguely related, but only vaguely so, as in a riddle. He feels a sense of mounting fear as he looks around the room. Perhaps it is the broken glass all about. Perhaps it is the trickle of blood flowing freely from his palm. And perhaps it is the other man: the brittle one. The views and histories of that party are even less distinct than his own. *There is no reason,* he says to himself, not entirely convinced, *to be afraid of* that *guy.*

Whenever they had previously met, he would always play the tough guy. The brittle man, being brittle, did his best to ignore him. Every act of toughness was met by the brittle man with an equal measure of yieldingness. The episodes always ended with the tough guy walking out first, puffed-up, strutting like a giant.

But today, the brittle man has gained the advantage. For the first time in their whole extended relationship, he is the one doing the talking.

"So," he asks, "who are you, really?"

The tough guy regards him sullenly.

"I'm you," he says.

He fumes, gripped with pain and rage over his demise. He did not mean to strike the mirror so hard, did not mean to smash it. All he had wanted was to crush that brittle face and silence it forever.

His hand throbs harder. The wound is still bleeding freely. It does not look as though it is going to stop.

II. Tattoo

At first, she wondered whether he might have lost his voice. Then she thought that perhaps he had chosen his silence as a show of solidarity: an attempt to unite with his fellow citizens in the communal pain of the military occupation.

In an occupied home, there was no freedom; only greater and lesser degrees of imprisonment.

So it was when they sent him home that numb winter night, naked and barefoot. They had found him guilty of two things, not enough to charge him with, but enough to prove his guilt: silence and that tattoo.

Silence opens the way to a grander space. It leaves you gasping and naked, your open wounds smarting with the salt of anticipation.

After a long silence, he spoke:

"With this," he tapped a finger against his head, "we can change the face of the world."

An anxious kind of joy coursed through her. She smiled.

At around eight o'clock the next morning, an unknown fist banged on the door, heralding the enraged swarm of bullets that poured forth from the walls and attacked him all at once, rendering him dead on the spot. She dropped to the floor like an olive tree broken by lightning, cradling his head in her hands, feeling his blood-warmed brains oozing through her fingers and onto his body, tattooing it with death.

The voiceless one, being silent, hears everything.

STAINED BY ROSES
Manal Hamdi

She had a habit of making rosewater and storing it in bottles in the fridge. As with most practices in which one has unwittingly become an expert, she enjoyed the process of making the stuff far more than she actually enjoyed drinking it. As a result, her fridge was brimming over with rosewater and she found herself offering it constantly to her guests.

On that ethereal night, which the hot, damp air inflated like a weather balloon, she was standing at the window when her visitor arrived, slamming the door behind him. The noise did not startle her. It only alerted her to his being there, so that she did not even have to turn her head around to acknowledge him. She was used to her visitors arriving at all hours of the day and the night. She knew their movements by heart, just like she knew by heart the taste of her rosewater. Everything went on as expected.

A little while later, she was shutting the window against the night, her head tilted back as she eyed her company with a practiced look of adoration. She mused over the quaint fixity of his gaze, his rose-tinted cheeks, the delicate ellipsoid of his mouth. She adopted a smile, camouflaging the boredom and disdain she felt toward him, and headed toward the bedroom. In a moment, she came back wearing a set of revealing lingerie, her hair spilling down over her shoulders. She knew this part by heart, too.

She paraded herself sensuously before her guest. Then she walked over to the fridge, opened it and, pulling out a fresh bottle of rosewater, poured the viscous bloodlike liquid, thick and fragrant, into a glass. She approached him, wafting the drink beneath his nose, grazing the rim of the glass against his lips, watching as beads of condensation gathered in an iridescent slick upon his cheek. All the while, she held her own face against the other side of the glass.

She stared at him in agony, waiting for him to move. She dragged the tips of her fingers over his chest, intoning tenderly,

"Why don't you let your chest hair grow out? When I caress a man's chest, I want to feel a *man's* chest. I want to feel aroused in return."

Then she upended the glass abruptly, pouring its contents over his hairless, childlike sternum. She drew nearer, as near as she could, embracing him fully: as though she were trying to fuse their two bodies together, filling in all of the remaining gaps between them.

But he did not move. He remained as a corpse, lifeless.

"Are you holding out on me?" she asked. "Why do you not talk, feel, sense, for God's sake! Am I not arousing you? Don't you want me to stay? Well then – what are you doing here?"

And so she carried on, indifferent to the silence of her guest, leaning over to plant a feverish kiss on his lips. Then she stood up, unfastening her bra – rose-stained, like everything else – with her left hand. She pulled it off and threw it into a corner. Now she was free.

She stretched out onto the sofa, fondling herself with both hands until she felt she was transformed into a human dynamo, charged and crackling with sex and its arcing desires.

She gasped and moaned. The electricity shot out of her in great bolts of rose-hued lightning. She moaned louder and her face stiffened, trembling, stuck in its rictus of pleasure, until finally her body relaxed from its *rigor petit-mortis* and she went limp. She felt her red-hot body sizzling and smoking as it was plunged into the annealing bath of fulfilled wants. But still, she wanted him. She devoured him with her eyes, inviting him silently to join her on the sofa.

He did not budge. She rolled over, her face to the couch-back, and fell asleep.

She woke up early the next morning, took a warm shower and dressed in the simple, unoffending garments of her day-trade. When she was done, she stood by the open window awhile, allowing her eyes an opportunity to wander over the morning's tableau. After a time, she withdrew from her reflections and shuffled back unenthusiastically to her seat at the sewing machine. She clenched her lips tightly over the brown thread, making sure it was moist before threading it minutely through the eye of a needle.

A customer arrived. (Her house, more than just a house, became, by the light of day, the workshop of a seamstress.)

The customer was talking:

73

"More rosewater, I see! Would it be presumptuous to think that this bottle is for me?"

"Not at all," the seamstress replied. "You are welcome to it."

"Oh, but," the customer said, glancing at the level of liquid inside, "this bottle's been drunk from! Should I get another from the fridge?"

"No," she said, smiling mysteriously. "This one is best. It's aged, sweet and smooth. Please take what's left."

"I will," said the customer, "thank you," slipping the bottle into her purse. "So are you done with my dress?"

"Yes," she nodded, "here it is."

The customer took the garment, draping it over her already-clothed figure and regarded herself in the mirror. She posed this way and that, curtsied and spun, and, in a moment, her foot snagged on the curtain, causing a manikin to topple to the floor with a dull clatter.

The seamstress jumped from her seat, fumbling with the light, corpselike figure. The customer clucked apologetically as she helped the seamstress set the manikin upright on its stand.

The customer withdrew her hand quickly as if she had just been burned.

"It's *sticky*," she exclaimed. She stood for a moment, mulling over her choice of words. "Say, what's the point of a men's manikin,

74

anyhow? I thought you only made clothing for women and children."

The seamstress stuttered a bit as she made her reply:

"I've… just started learning how to make a man's suit." She paused. "Who knows? I might even open a proper shop someday, God willing."

"Yes," the other woman said, responding in kind. "God willing!"

RAIN
Musa Abu Rayash

His tired feet guided him backwards down the path. So turned around was he, that he could barely comprehend his direction. His heart was heavy, his innards black with despair. He had sundered every chance to improve his life – to pull himself out of that shitty job that paid him only enough such that he would not end up on the street with the rabble. He thanked God that he was a single person without spousal or paternal obligations.

My life is hard, he thought, *but at least my responsibilities end with myself.*

Suddenly, his ears picked up a distress signal: a weeping child, somewhere close. He scanned the street until he spotted a little girl sitting on the threshold of one of the houses, crying her eyes out. He made his way toward her, his apprehension melting quickly in the warm, pellucid innocence of the child's whimpering. Glimmering pearls rolled off her cheeks and turned to water as they made landfall on the street. He thought she resembled nothing so much as a wayward angel who had taken her refuge, inexplicably, inside the body of this child.

He felt his soul ignite with the fire of compassion; and the fire threw off its sweet perfumes: happiness, hope, affection. He squatted before her, raised his eyebrows disarmingly and asked:

"Why are you crying, my dear?"

She did not answer, but only kept on crying. He repeated the question. She answered brokenly:

"I want... ch-chocolate... Like the o-o-other kids. But... but... I have n-no money!"

He asked her about her parents. Did they not give her money for chocolate?

But her father was dead, she said, and her mother had gone away to look for a job.

He took her by the hand and lifted her gently from the ground. Tears sparkled on her cheeks like divinely crafted gems. He took her to the nearest grocery counter and bought her all the sweets her little heart desired, paying the clerk with a heap of small change that he pulled from his pockets. They walked back together to her home, the girl leading the way.

At the door of the house, he stopped her and, taking her arm, spoke to her in a pious tone of what had transpired between them today. If it had not been for the furtive glances of the people in the street, he would have stayed with her until her mother arrived. But he could not. He bid her goodbye and walked away, back to his part of town, without so much as a backward glance. To stay with her would have meant surrendering to the inevitable misunderstandings, the blindness, that shockingly unjust interpretation of adult male kindness which sprang so quickly to people's minds that it had become a sort of awful cliché: to surrender to these things was to surrender the very treasure he had acquired today. No: he was determined to keep this treasure for himself. He went on his way rejoicing and possessed with a newfound alacrity that gave him the sense of flying.

He arrived at his home and went inside quickly, joyfully. He tore off his heavy, soiled clothes and dove headlong into the rude succor of a workingman's bed. For the first time, as he recalled the image of his little, lachrymose angel, he felt the sense that there was actually such a thing as beauty in the world – the kind of beauty that endowed existence with the sweet fragrance of joy and happiness; that made life, despite its darkness and barbarity, into something worthy of being lived.

Things changed for him after that. He approached his work with a zeal and dedication unrivalled among his colleagues. The supervisor, impressed with his "commitment to seriousness and integrity," awarded him a bonus, then a raise. Rewards and achievements accrued to him and he was content. He made friends and, in the nourishing light of friendship, his heart blossomed anew: for the first time in a long time, he actually felt it beating. He rediscovered a confidence that he had not had since childhood. In his sleep, he made a continuous pilgrimage to the teeming wilderness of his dreams, charting with each passing night the topography of that vast, rugged continent.

His dreams brought him visions of a new life: marriage, a spacious house, loving children; children with faces halfway like his own. He especially dreamed of children. And so he set to preparing for this future as he envisioned it: boiling down his thoughts into plans and projects, ruling out certain possibilities, repurposing others, until a complete and perfect image of it crystallized in his mind. This image lived within him for many nights, buoying his mind and his mood above the surface of everyday affairs. Sometimes, he even felt as though the everyday was the phantasm and that the glorious, but as-yet unripe, future was, in fact, his present reality.

One late, September day, as he was making his way home from work, the sky burst open, signaling the start of the rainy season. Children burst forth in turn, flowing in multihued torrents of gaiety and wonder, from every house on every street, flocking to one another like a dole of doves, as they welcomed the rain with a single voice:

> *Come on, rain! Pour down, rain!*
> *Our house has got a thick steel frame.*
> *Abdullah is my uncle's name*
> *and Allah makes our bread from grain.*

The children ran through the streets, embracing the rain ecstatically with their sinless bodies, catching raindrops in their open mouths. The lovesick ground, refulgent and damp, exuded the unmistakable scent of its intimate encounter with the sky. The people observed all of these conflagrant joys with a sigh of relief.

"Thanks be to God," they uttered. "Praise be to God."

He felt his spirit buoying him up into the air with the rest of the children. His bosom opened to receive the rain's generosity. He felt the defilements of his body washed away under the baptismal showers that descended from the sky in exquisite, shining columns. He pulled off his jacket and tie, kicked off his shoes, and ran into the throng of children singing and playing. In a single, deft movement, he shrugged away the cynical eyes that deployed his behavior; sneering lips that muttered and backbit.

80

The rest were cowards, he realized: cowards masquerading in the garb of heroes. The rest were too brittle to bend his way, to return themselves, as he had, to the Pure Land, the Country of the Innocent – even for a few moments, for the duration of a cloudburst! – electing, instead, to remain as they were:

Prisoners within themselves.

EYES CONFUSED
Khalid Yousef Abu Tamaa

I t is a quiet place, this place that once was – not long ago, but not any longer, either – filled with the aroma of pipe tobacco. And we see him walking through it toward the table. He is walking with confidence, impervious to the swarm of suspicious glances that steals at him from every corner table and bench, from every able socket.

She is a lady in her 50s, unafflicted by any signs of apparent aging, no wrinkles, nothing, that could give away her true age. And there she sits, looking reverent and magnificent at her table. Anyone would have said that she was at the height of her splendor, radiating serenity and adorned with a confidence unspoiled by her pride.

He takes a seat opposite the table from her, allowing his attention to roam for a minute around the room, and, content that everyone is minding their own business, he lets his attention settle on her at last. He is just sitting there, staring into those wide, piercing eyes; staring at her in silence as though the act has somehow deprived him of his capacity for speech.

He summons intelligence and wisdom and they come slowly, petulant servants that they are, until they bring him the words he is looking for:

"What is your name?"

Listen now: the low purr of bubbling hookahs rises in a dull wave until it envelops the place. Now smell: the room refulgent with tobacco smoke, each billowing cloud pregnant with the tiny, beating wings of a thousand desires, floating in the air like so many butterflies!

She breathes a sigh of relief and, with a peaceful smile and a look of deep reverence, she says:

"Wafa.[2] My name is Wafa Abdul Rahman."

He cannot contain himself. He has to smile. Wafa is the name of the protagonist in his first novel. It is also the name of an old friend of his: one who is long dead, but who lives on vividly in his memories, the old ones, the important ones – the ones he swears he will never lose.

The great thrills and disasters, the lessons and achievements, of those times have always been a source of satisfaction, even solace, to him. We should not be surprised that some of his measures to preserve his memories, to keep them from slipping down the Teflon-covered walls of life, were to manifest themselves in ham-fisted ploys such as the one in which now he finds himself.

All these things are running through his mind as he sits there staring into her eyes: staring quite rudely, in fact, or it would have been rude if her gaze had not been fixed in exactly the same manner upon his own coffee-colored visage. Clouds of butterfly-smoke drift between them and her melodious voice steers nimbly in turn through them.

---

[2] A common female name meaning "loyalty."

I must, he insists thoughtfully to himself, *I must keep eye contact.*

Meanwhile, she is talking:

"Tell me, have you ever even walked into someplace like this before? Does it make you feel uneasy, being here?

"I've never sat here with someone like you – a man, that is. And this table has been booked for me a long time, you know.

"This place is packed with suckers, don't you see? People fuming against their hookahs, people possessed by blurred visions and secret hearts.

"I don't know why you— ah.

"You just tickle my fancy. You give me hope in something that's been missing for a long time.

"Are you still taken with your old habits? Do you still write? I wonder about you writers.

"I wonder: Why do you do it? What's the point of draining your soul into a pen and your mind into an inkwell, if nobody cares for what you have to say?

"Do you think that everyone in this room is happy? Or – if not everyone – at least everyone else?"

She does not even stop; she answers her own question:

"I don't think so. Everybody pretends to be happy, but they do it in such boring, obviously unhappy, ways. Here they are, playing the role of a happy professional. Here they are, playing the role of a skillful devotee of some art. But eventually all of us must acknowledge our failure. Nobody's happy playing one narrow role.

"Some people, many people, think that happiness is something to be bought and sold, with money perhaps. But look at me! I've got plenty of money and I still couldn't tell you which of the market-stalls would best furnish you with happiness.

"Money doesn't buy the compassion I'd like to feel. It can't buy the tenderness I crave from those around me, nor a sense of belonging among those who belong to me.

"I always end up bitter. Then I have no choice – but to yield to my own entropy."

Her composure instills in him a dual feeling, simultaneous, of great wonder and confusion. In a moment, though, the first signs of concern appear on her face; her hands and lips tremble like a dam before bursting.

He keeps looking into her face. He is listening to what she has to say, damn it. He clothes himself with silence and thoughtfulness, vowing that each word he utters will become, like hers, a fountain of pure fragrance as it leaves his lips:

"In nature, every action leaves its mark.

"And yes, this place is unfamiliar to me. I see no mark of mine here.

"And no, I could never quit my habit of writing. My pen is the true governor of that province of life and it writes whatever it wishes, whenever it wishes; always wanting to state my opinion on some such thing. But I've learned that the only way to deal with this tyrant is to surround him with walls: the highest and sturdiest walls one can erect. Nobody can control such a thing, but one can imprison it.

"And yes, at the end of the day, we writers tend either to be neglected or forgotten – so why should I worry about it! Happiness is real and its inner workings are the truest source of beauty.

"Every bit of happiness brings on its coattails a little parcel of love and an equal measure of generosity. A person can't live by bread alone *or* by money alone.

"This isn't a philosophy, my lady. This is a fact.

"All of us find ourselves, at some point in life, in the unpleasant depths of privation. The wealthy are hounded by their wealth, just as the poor are hounded by their needs.

"When one feels love from those close to him, then he has gotten back some of his own affection from the great pool of human kindness.

"When you give without any sense of reciprocity, you're at the peak of your loyalty. Few indeed are those who can live without yearning for the love they've given away."

He pauses in his speech. Her face bespeaks grief, yet he is not sure how it got there. He wonders what it was that he said, if it even was something that he said, but he cannot begin to fathom the depths of her mind. Is there some underlying secret there, one that he might use, like a strange and mythical weapon forged in the arcane smithy of his enemy, to wipe the misery from her beautiful face? His words so far have seemed to dispel her anxieties, but...

Oh. Now his phone is ringing. He looks down at it, the contours of his face shifting subtly, but not imperceptibly. He drains the remaining coffee from his cup, flags down the waiter, pays and tips.

Now it is just the table in the scene before us: the way it was moments ago, smoke-clouds and all, except for our lonely pair. They have left the place hurriedly, stepping out into the open air, those old, tattered melancholies drawn snugly over their faces.

BIG FANG
Julnar Zain

The sun, as usual, takes advantage of her somnolence, sending its rays to creep over her angelic, sleeping face. The goldfinch, however, being more of a terrestrial creature than the sun on its far-off throne, is aware that for the young lady, today is different. And so he dares to sing right from the headboard of her bed, rather than take up his usual perch on the louver across the room.

Today is the first day of spring, the day when the moon in its fullness takes on the aspect of a gigantic pearl in the sky, illuminating the road for all the night-spirits, those confused souls, of the damned earth; to guide them in their blind search for eternal serenity. Or, at least, so say the legends.

Our beautiful, young sleeper is stirring. The spark of cognition shines through her heavy-lidded eyes. We can see that, in addition to her exquisite beauty, our maiden is blessed with both ample spirit and a sharpness of wit… although it would be dishonest to say that these qualities are not totally eclipsed by her breathtaking physical appeal. As it should be with our heroine – what kind of woman needs strength or intelligence for herself, when all the strength and intelligence she needs can be provided by men? The stronger sex, the more intelligent sex, certainly has enough of such qualities to go around.

The maiden takes her time combing her hair. Now she dresses herself, pulling on the sumptuous regalia reserved for the daughter of a sheikh. Go on, admire her beauty some more:

watch as she steps out of her father's house to join the happy crowds gathering for the springtime rites. She surveys the village square, thinking of all the things she will do today.

The fiancé of our maiden, taking advantage of the preoccupation of his betrothed, collides with her deliberately and steals a kiss – quite possibly, too passionate a kiss – for we can see that her cheeks flush with color before she pushes him gently away.

"Whoa, there," she says, "get a hold on yourself! Our wedding day will be here soon enough."

Her fiancé says nothing. What is there to say? He finds her disposition maddeningly coquettish. He wishes that he could perch on her headboard – screw that wretched goldfinch! – and greet the morning alongside her.

The maiden waves to him as she walks away, joining the other women in their preparations for the springtime rites.

It'll be a riotous springtime, she thinks to herself as she ties, somewhat absentmindedly, a very pretty wildflower onto a chain of its compatriots. *An unparalleled springtime, this year.*

In the midst of these harmless preoccupations, her father, the Sheikh, passes her amid the crowd. He beams at his lovely daughter, sending clandestine rays of pure love and pride – and possibly some other emotion, although what this might be is not yet apparent – to creep over her angelic face.

As the day wears on into night, the people of the village flock to the arena to witness the ceremony. Young women sway and warble to the beat of the drum. Baskets of food and flowers, trinkets and sweets, pass from hand to hand. In short order, dozens of the maiden's hand-woven daisy chains adorn the necks of the villagers.

On stage, in the royal gallery behind the podium of the Sheikh, the beautiful young lady basks in the electric delight of the crowd. Her fiancé, his cheeks flushed from drink, approaches her. With one hand, he proffers a chalice of blackberry juice.

"I made it myself," he declares. "For you, my dear."

Taking the chalice, our maiden raises it gently to her smiling lips – but before she can imbibe any of the liquid, a hideous insect touches down, sending minute ripples and splashes over the surface of the drink until, finally, the creature is submerged and sinks. The maiden recoils from the chalice in horror and, taking advantage of her fiancé's preoccupation with the dancing girls onstage, empties her drink discreetly into the rose bushes planted along the wall.

I should keep this incident to myself, she muses, examining the chalice for bits of drowned insect. *I wouldn't want to hurt his feelings...*

He looks back from the dancers, beaming as he glances from her face to the empty chalice in her hand. Various feelings of guilt wash over her.

Am I, she thinks, *being too deceptive to my husband-to-be?*

If only she knew – *she's* the one being deceived!

The tumult diminishes along a slow decrescendo. One of the village elders is rising from his seat; he is clapping his hands, he is calling out, over the rapt faces of the crowd:

"It's time! ...*It's time!*"

The beautiful maiden cannot quite comprehend what is now beginning to happen. Everything is blurry. People crowd around her, snarling and roaring like wild animals. The young men have pounced on her and are tying her up: that is right. They have trussed her up like a lamb on the temple steps and she is bleating furiously as any rational person would do, beseeching her ladies-in-waiting for help; crying out to her father for help, but they seem to not notice her. They turn their backs, she glances around frantically for her fiancé; he is not in the crowd, where is he?

He is standing over her, tying the final knot that will hold her arms against her back.

"What are you doing," she yells, her innocence bound with the harsh cables of betrayal. "Why are you helping these men?"

"I'm sorry, darling," he says, his face rigid, his apology hollow; his reflexive *darling* implying no emotional connection whatsoever. "But you are this year's oblation to Big Fang."

They set out, the fiancé and two of his male companions, dragging her behind on a sled. They drag her deep into the forest, past the boundaries of her father's village, beyond the pale into No Man's Land, whose name was such because no man would dare lay claim to it unless it was certain death they sought.

After a time, they come upon a clearing of sorts amid which sits a sorry, decrepit stump. They lead her to it and sit her down, still bound. The fiancé kneels and whispers into her ear:

"Don't worry, you won't feel a thing. The juice you drank earlier – it was drugged."

With that, two other young men and himself withdraw into the forest and head back to the village, eager to rejoin the celebration – or rather, to re-enliven it – and content in the fulfillment of their duty, having now given the maiden the appropriate solitude in which to contemplate her fears.

Meanwhile, our maiden is fiddling with the knots against her wrist, wrenching against the knots between her shoulders, squirming against the knots between her ankles. She fiddles with them all until one reveals its promise and comes undone, then another and another finally, until she rises from the rude, rotting pedestal unbound.

They must not have been trying too hard to contain me, she muses. *Of course, they also think I'm drugged.*

It occurs to her that Big Fang might know better.

Every child who grows up in the presence of stories has grown up knowing and fearing Big Fang. She had heard the stories herself, but did not fear him. She knew that, just like any other mythical forest-goblins and mountain-djinns, conjured and sent forth by parents in order to scare some obedience into their children, Big Fang did not exist.

But wait: there is a rustle in the undergrowth. Something is moving toward her. She can make out its heavy footfalls, its labored breathing.

"Lord, have mercy," she breathes, her eyes wide with fear.

This must be the end, she thinks. *This is how I die.* And then...*but with God as witness, I won't die without a fight!*

The creature steps into the clearing, lambent in the moonlight. The jaw of the maiden drops.

The creature is ancient, decrepit, old and wrinkled; its mangy skin draped like loose fabric over a creaky, withered tent-frame. All that is left of his eponymous tooth is a ground-down, yellowed stump that protrudes from his upper jaw, like some oddly complimentary jigsaw piece to the stump upon which her captors had left her.

Is this, she wonders, *his 'lethal fang?' He can't be hiding another under there!*

...The creature, meanwhile, approaches her menacingly, although with evidently geriatric clumsiness...

Well, she thinks, *it appears Big Fang is real. But ferocious and dangerous? I think not. A child half my size could knock down this ol' bag of bones!*

...the creature is closing in now, extending a trembling claw towards her neck, but in an instant she ducks and rolls out of the way. The creature advances again, the maiden letting it trail her by no more and no less than a single beast-stride, always out of

94

its grasp. She is wearing him down. The creature slows, perhaps with exasperation, and it is at this exact moment that the maiden produces from her clothing an ordinary, tapered shiv – a piece of wood sufficient for hunting nothing more threatening than a fly – and reaches in beneath the creature's cramped and brittle chest, stabbing him in the heart. He bleeds out quickly, drops to the ground like some dried-out husk of a plant. As if dislodged by the force of life leaving his body, the gnarled, diminished stump of a fang flies from his mouth and lands next to her with a pitiful *thud*.

The creature appears to be dead, but she needs to be certain, nudging it with her toe. That is certainty enough. She picks the fang off the ground and rushes back in the direction of the village.

Surely, she thinks, *they'll be elated by the news I've brought them!*

Sometime later, she arrives back in town. The crowds are still milling about: chanting, dancing, feasting.

Is this, she wonders, her mouth agape, *a celebration of my death?*

There, across the amphitheater and beyond the dais, she sees him. Her fiancé – or, rather, her ex-fiancé because he is sitting now with a new bride, newly wedded.

I've only been gone half a day, she thinks, *and my betrothed has already remarried? Is this how he deals with heartbreak?*

The village, as she is now finding out, has not missed her one bit. She stands in the center of the amphitheater, gazing out at them. All voices diminish into silence. Her father runs out at her like a madman, waving his arms, cursing into her face:

95

"What have you done?!" He wrests the creature's fang from her grasp, repeating, "What have you *done?!* You've brought shame and destruction upon our people!"

She turns to her ladies in waiting, but they spit and swear at her:

"You should be dead, you contemptible, selfish coward!"

Out of the crowd, the ex-fiancé approaches, takes the fang deftly out of the Sheikh's still-outstretched hand and pivots around to stab the maiden in her gut, in a single, sudden movement. She falls, doubled over, radiating pain. With tremendous effort, she lifts her head, staring to understand her father's actions, which despite her present agony she cannot ignore. She speaks just as her father finishes ordering his guards, to deploy into the wild:

"But, Father! I killed the monster. I killed Big Fang! We've been released from our captivity!"

The Sheikh turns and regards her coolly:

"Fool of a daughter! My men aren't going out there to save little girls like you. I sent them out there," he's smiling now, "to look for a new monster."

ABOUT IBTIHAL MAHMOOD

Ibtihal Mahmood is a Jordanian translator, journalist and poet. She was born in Kuwait, then moved to Jordan with her family after the Gulf war in 1990. She attended the University of Jordan at Amman, graduating with a B.A. in English literature in 2005. In November 2013, Mahmood became the chairperson of the Arabic Division of the International Medical Interpreters Association (IMIA). She is also a member of the American Translators Association (ATA) and the American Literary Translators Association (ALTA).

Mahmood's poetry has appeared in many international anthologies, including the *Premio Mondiale Poesia Nosside* in Reggio Calabria, Italy. Recently, Ibtihal revived her love for journalistic writing and joined the list of contributors at *The Seattle Globalist*, an award-winning daily publication covering the connection between Seattle and the rest of the globe. Presently, Mahmood is an M.A. candidate in Middle Eastern Studies at the University of Washington. She lives in Seattle, Washington.

ABOUT ALEXANDER HADDAD

Alexander Haddad is an American poet, writer and editor. He is the founder and former executive director of *Old Growth Northwest*, a community and advocacy organization for poets and writers living in the Pacific Northwest. His work on *Snow in Amman* reflects his long-standing love affair with the literature and culture of the Near East, as well as a fascination with his own Levantine roots.

As an undergraduate at Georgetown University, Haddad studied Arabic language and literature, together with his degree in Contemporary American Studies. His undergraduate capstone project – an original, allegorical novel paired with a "skeleton key" style exegesis – was awarded the *2009 Mary Catherine Mita Prize for Outstanding Undergraduate Thesis*. Haddad has received numerous other awards for his writing, including a National Silver Medal in nonfiction by *The New York Times/Alliance for Arts & Writing*. He lives in Portland, Oregon.

SELECTED FARAXA PUBLICATIONS

#1 UK Bestseller **Known to Social Services** by senior child protection worker Freya Barrington. Written from life experience and ringing with authenticity, the book follows Diane Foster into the grim, grey world of the Deacon Hill estate in Millbrook. Domestic violence, child abuse, serial paedophiles and ex-convicts proliferate in the daily lives of most of the children, but Diane enters deeply into this world of misery to help the victims and keep together the fragile structure of society. Hampered by an administration inhabited by paper-shuffling and uninvolved, uncaring bureaucrats, Diane fights to protect the children of Deacon Hill from rape, horror, random violence, female genital mutilation and murder, in context of a horrifying barrenness and desolate existential reality.

Bonds in the Mirror of Time is a psychological novel by Rena Balzan, Ph.D., translated from the Maltese by Antoinette Pace. Love and selfishness continually compete with each other, dominating the protagonists. Why was Nada abandoned by her mother? Who was Maris? Why was Claud dating her when he loved Nada? The painter, a very reserved individual, was afraid to fulfil himself as an artist. Why did he end his relationship with Erica, the woman who desired to help him succeed? In this novel, the human bonding that exists between the

main protagonists is not necessarily annihilated by death. On the contrary, the psychological barriers death portrays present a challenge for overcoming them.

Ittra lil Tarbija li Qatt Ma Twieldet / Lettera a Un Bambino Mai Nato by the Italian journalist and author Oriana Fallaci, translated into Maltese by Christine Bajada.

The Legend of Amanda Robins is a supernatural thriller for young adults by teenage Maltese-American author Corrine Annette Zahra. It is a fast-moving, gripping account of the turmoil resulting from the destruction of Magic State, an invisible island north of Australia. Queen Amanda is forced to evacuate her land and send the inhabitants to live with humankind. Her ex-husband, Dylan, has escaped from a prison island with hordes of werewolves and launched a vicious attack. From the streets of New York where new Twin Towers are born, to the White House, Queen Amanda puts all her powers on display. War and intrigue permeate the pages of Zahra's book which should prove un-put-downable for lovers of magical creatures.

A Land in the Storytelling Sea – A North American in Malta by Sheryl Loeffler presents 50 poems and 50 full-colour, original photographs of the Maltese Islands. Sensual, painterly, even prayerful, these poems and pictures deepen into a land of legend and myth; an island populated, past and present, by saints, beggars and pirates, all of whom are blessed by vivid geometries of light. Loeffler portrays Malta as a country awash in splendor and contradiction, a

"land where Christians call God *Alla*." This book is quietly pleasurable in its narrative journey and in its subtle, seductive craft.

Dinjet il-Qattus / Catlore is the Maltese language edition of the famous book by the zoologist and ethologist Desmond Morris, translated by Toni Aquilina, D. es L.

The Battle Roar of Silence – Foucault and the Carceral System by Meinrad Calleja explores the philosophical rationales sustaining morality, law, punishment and the carceral system as part of the globalization discourse. He desacralizes the foundations of this discourse using Foucault's archaeological and genealogical study of institutions, knowledge, discourse and power. Calleja fuses sociological and psychoanalytical aspects in a philosophical framework, to tender a politically-charged critique of contemporary modes of domination and power. Calleja correlates the carceral system discourse to political, social and economic antagonisms that have eroded human rights, democracy and freedom. Consumers of this discourse repress the negative features of such a despotic order and suffer in silence.

Popular Operas in the Maltese Islands by Maltese, award-winning author Tony C. Cutajar presents the 20 most favorite operas from the time they started being produced in Malta and Gozo up to 2012. Interesting details about each opera and its composer are given, with plot summaries. Interactive links to audio/video selections of the best arias are also provided in the ebook edition of this book.

Bormla – A Struggling Community is a landmark study in which JosAnn Cutajar, Ph.D., presents the people's situation in this impoverished, historical, Maltese city. Communities living in places stigmatized by policy makers, the media and the general population, develop coping skills to acquire alternative resources for their social well-being. In Maltese society, resources are often deployed by policy and decision makers not cognizant of the differential needs of communities living in different places. Cutajar gives voice to the people of Bormla, bringing their needs to the forefront and giving effective recommendations for change.

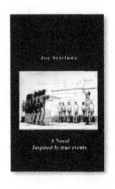

Ricasoli Soldier – A Novel Inspired by True Events by Joe Scicluna presents Leo Bonanno, a young man who left Sicily in 1806 to enlist as a soldier with the British Army in Malta. The British had just formed the new regiment and recruited many from Albania, Greece, Italy, Russia and Turkey. But the recruitment process was fraudulent. Leo held many hopes, dreams and ambitions of youth, including the desire to become a soldier to better serve his country. Stationed at Fort Ricasoli in Malta, he made new friends and fell madly in love with Lisa, a beautiful village girl from Kalkara. But all Leo's hopes, dreams and ambitions rapidly turned into a terrifying nightmare and incomparable battle for survival, due to a system of iniquity imposed by a major who was a heartless tyrant.

Strange Tales by Charles Coyne is a collection of 29 horror stories, many of which are set in the Maltese Islands. Ranging from Max the doll who ends up being a preternatural killer, through Meinertzhagen the man who turns into a boy after death who tries to entrap his best friend, to Loki the shaman who visits with the dead, Coyne manifests himself a true master at sleight of hand in these tales. Coyne keeps his readers on edge, gripping the seat of their chairs, both during the telling of the tales and in their surprise endings.

Escape – A Supernatural Serial by Corrine Zahra is for young adults. I am Tiffany Crooks and with my little sister, Minnie, I live at *The Turville's* with Grandma Crooks and her family. But who are the Crooks and the Turvilles? Why does Grandma Crooks desire to consecrate my sister with blood to the dark sacred even though we are Christians? Who is the flame-flickered hound? Above all, why did our parents suddenly disappear after they dropped us off with Grandma Crooks? Where are they now when Minnie and I most need them? Help! What is going to happen to us?

The Philosophy of Desert Metaphors in Ibrahim al-Koni – The Bleeding of the Stone by Meinrad Calleja looks closely at one of al-Koni's works and prises out philosophical reflections concealed in the text. A Tuareg by birth, al-Koni's works have earned international repute and academic recognition. Themed around a desert context, his novels are post-modern, polyphonic, magical or socialist realism and Sufi fabula. Calleja shows how the desert provides a landscape rich in allusions, while metaphors facilitate creative interpretation.

Il-Litteratura fit-Traduzzjoni / Literature in Translation by the Department of Translation, Terminology and Interpreting Studies of the University of Malta. Contains works in English, Italian and Maltese by Borge, Camus, de Unamuno, Friggieri, Fussenegger, Hardy, Lawrence, Meilak, Moravia and Somerset Maugham.

L-Alla tal-Ħerba / Le Dieu du Carnage by the award-winning author Yasmina Reza, translated into Maltese by Toni Aquilina, D. es L.

Stories My Parents Told Me – Tales of Growing Up in Wartime Malta by Maltese-Australian author Rupert C. Grech are based on actual events during WWII in Malta. Grech skillfully shows the difficult time it was for children and families where survival was paramount and family ties were what sustained them. The stories are interspersed with snippets of history, factual details and settings for tales emotionally moving, some of which bring a smile to your face. Grech also describes a culture of a time past for a deeply religious, frugal people.

In Her Element – Poems by award-winning author Therese Pace presents a collection of 60 poems which address the daily vicissitudes of modern life with the fluidity and skill of a master. From *Garden Dwarf* to*Growing Tall,* to *Orizons of a Disgruntled Citizen* and beyond, Pace employs the mighty power of words to convey an unlimited source of expression and emotions. Called "an artisan of the word, a craftswoman, a wordsmith," Pace presents words that go beyond utterance and meaning, generating a long-lasting echo in the reader's heart, mind and soul.

Is-Sajf / L'Eté by Nobel prizewinner Albert Camus, translated into Maltese by Toni Aquilina, D. es L.

Is-Sur Ibrahim u l-Fjuri fil-Koran / Monsieur Ibrahim et Les Fleurs du Coran by Eric-Emmanuel Schmitt, translated into Maltese by Toni Aquilina, D. es L.

Il-Ħajja u l-Avventuri ta' Santa Klaws / The Life and Adventures of Santa Claus by Frank L. Baum, translated into Maltese by Matthew Scerri, Ph.D.

Meaulnes it-Twil / Les Grand Meaulnes by Henri Alain-Fournier, translated into Maltese by Paul Zahra.

Made in the USA
Monee, IL
30 January 2023

26719435R00059